New York Athenæum association

Commemorative Proceedings of the Athenáeum Club

on the death of Abraham Lincoln, president of the United States

New York Athenæum association

Commemorative Proceedings of the Athenáeum Club
on the death of Abraham Lincoln, president of the United States

ISBN/EAN: 9783337402556

Printed in Europe, USA, Canada, Australia, Japan

Cover: Foto ©Andreas Hilbeck / pixelio.de

More available books at **www.hansebooks.com**

COMMEMORATIVE PROCEEDINGS

OF THE

ATHENÆUM CLUB,

ON THE DEATH OF

ABRAHAM LINCOLN,

PRESIDENT OF THE UNITED STATES.

·

APRIL, 1865.

PROCEEDINGS

ATHENÆUM CLUB.

—··— — —

AT the written request of several members of the Association, an informal meeting was held at the Club House, on the evening of the 18th day of April, 1865.

The President. Mr. WILLIAM T. BLODGETT, in calling the meeting to order, addressed the members as follows:

GENTLEMEN: The members of the Athenæum Club have assembled this evening under circumstances of the most painful and distressing character. A National Calamity has befallen us which has no parallel in the history of the world in modern times. Our representative head has been stricken down by the hand of an assassin, in the hour of our country's regeneration, and has turned a nation's joy and ju-

4

bilee into a nation's grief and woe. We have met this evening to take such action as may be meet and proper to give expression to the feelings of this Club, at the Great Calamity which has befallen us all in the loss of our wise ruler and that good man, ABRAHAM LINCOLN, President of the United States. Let us, as a Club, give expression to our grief, and mingle our sympathies with those of our common country.

On motion of Mr. T. BAILEY MYERS, the following resolution was unanimously adopted:

Resolved; That a Committee of seven be appointed by the Chair to propose and submit to the Club, resolutions expressive of the profound grief felt by its members at the loss the country has sustained in the assassination of the President of the United States.

The following gentlemen were designated to compose such Committee:

T. BAILEY MYERS, *Chairman,*

FRANCIS A. STOUT,	GEORGE P. PUTNAM,
HENRY T. TUCKERMAN,	JOHN H. PLATT,
W. CARY SMITH,	RICHARD WINNE.

On motion of Mr. JOHN A. C. GRAY, it was

Resolved; That a Committee be appointed to communicate with the authorities, and make such arrangements as will enable the Club to participate in any funeral obsequies that may be instituted in honor of the late President.

The Chair announced the following Committee of Arrangements:

JOHN A. C. GRAY, *Chairman.*

JAS. H. VAN ALEN, HORACE M. RUGGLES,
WILLIAM S. CONSTANT, SCHUYLER SKAATS.
W. GRACIE ULLSHOEFFER, JOHN H. PROUT.

Captain CHARLES PYNE suggested that we should recommend to the Art Committee to secure, from one of the Artist Members, a portrait of the late President, to be hung in the Club-House. This suggestion was approved.

On motion, the meeting adjourned to meet on the following evening to receive the reports of the Committees.

GEORGE V. N. BALDWIN,
Secretary.

April 19th, 1865.

Pursuant to adjournment, the Club assembled at 8 o'clock, P. M., the President in the Chair. The proceedings of the previous meeting were read and approved.

Mr. T BAILEY MYERS, Chairman of the Committee on Resolutions, prefaced their introduction with the following remarks:

MR. PRESIDENT: The duty has been devolved upon me of submitting to the Club resolutions feebly expressing our sympathy in this great National Bereavement. It would appear eminently proper that we should participate in the public grief over our fallen leader. We have sympathized in his struggles, have appreciated his exertions and his sacrifices, and now that he has crowned them with his life, it is just that we should lay our humble tribute on his bloody tomb. We all recollect how doubtfully his first Inauguration was received, how many of us distrusted his ability to cope with the Southern people, goaded into a bitter hatred of the North, under the lash of their unscrupulous leaders. We remember, too, how the heart of the Nation rose when he proclaimed that the Unity of the States should be preserved. We had doubted, under the feeble Administration of his predecessor, whether we were a Nation or a temporary consolidation of communities, to be broken at will by any factions member. We realized, when the cannon thundered before Sumpter, that we still possessed the love of country and the disposition to save it at any cost, which were necessary to insure that end. We had rung conciliation, compromise, and concession, through all their phases; had hesitated at coercion, but now we recognized subjugation, if necessary, as preferable to annihilation, held one more Union-saving meeting, threw down the olive-branch and drew the sword. Party preferences forgotten, a whole people rushed to arms and accepted ABRAHAM LINCOLN as their leader.

Clubs are little worlds in themselves, each member brings to a common centre his prejudices and his sympathies, his intelligence in discussion, and his candor in accepting conviction. The Clubs of New York, as organized bodies of intelligent men, at once became the centre of Patriotic activity, and much good was done in those early days, and many a man buckled on his sword, took up his pen, or arrayed himself actively and usefully in the great cause, inspired by the convictions ripened by Club discussion.

The Athenæum, Sir, was not behind in this great work, and she can point with pride to a long list of members who have done good service in the field, in the study, or in the councils of the nation.

We can recall how intently those who found no better opportunity in active exertion, watched the struggle and followed the progress of our armies with their flag-markers on the map, as they slowly progressed on the borders of the dark region of Secession, grand enough to form the area of an Empire, dark enough for the antechamber of Hades. The news from the army was received with intense anxiety; we mourned over their reverses, we rejoiced in their triumphs; we fought their battles over again, canvassed private information and public reports, and sometimes accepted probabilities for results and rumors for facts, often to be disappointed. We had our favorite generals, and our prejudices against generals, and discussed the merits of Butler (first in the field), McClellan, Fremont, McDowell, Pope, Burnside, Rosecrans, Sherman, Thomas, Sheridan, and Grant, as each in turn assumed a prominent place. Perhaps we had a stronger bias for our own three Major-Generals in the field, and a warmer desire that opportunity should be given to them than to others, not only because they were Athenæum men, but

because they had distinguished themselves in many
a desperate struggle. Nor were our naval heroes
overlooked in the councils of the Club, or their
brilliant achievements forgotten. With them to en-
gage was to succeed, and a battle was almost in-
variably a victory.

Perhaps these easy-chair criticisms of more earnest
patriots, who fought and suffered while we were
discussing their efforts in a peaceful seclusion from
the din of battle, to which we were indebted to
their valor, might argue indifference to the mighty
events which were passing around us; but while it
was not possible for all to participate, it is but
just to believe that many reluctantly accepted in-
action as a necessity. To discuss and to read the
newspapers are pure American characteristics. The
deliberations of the Athenæum were but typical of
those of all circles at home, and of the Cabinets and
people of every civilized nation of the globe. The
institutions of a mighty nation were on their trial,
and the question of self-government to be passed
upon. Well might those not battling for them
watch and pray!

Meanwhile, four years were dragging slowly on.
The hand on the dial seemed leaden in its
course. The hope of peace, often apparently near
at hand, still intangible and remote.

In all this period there was a patient, hopeful, earnest man, gifted with a clear perception and an honest, patriotic heart, struggling at the national capital, often within sound of the enemy's cannon, at once the ruler and the servant of the people. To him, years were but as days in preserving the life of the nation; he stopped at no labor, he complained of no fatigue, he shunned no responsibility; his only recreation seemed to be the indulgence of a quaint humor in an occasional epigram or joke, which served to show how light his heart was in his good work. We have heard of no jokes made by Jefferson Davis in the course of this war. He has lived to realize in the very existence of his paper fabric of a confederacy the saddest burlesque of the century.

The exertions of Mr. Lincoln, and the immense labors thrown upon him in those years, those who have witnessed them can scarcely realize, and they will be but faintly portrayed when the history of the struggle is written. He had to organize a government, an army, a navy, a treasury, to select his co-laborers, to reconcile their jealousies, to harmonize discordant factions, to satisfy grasping place-seekers, to decide on such vexed questions of policy at home and abroad, as had never been passed upon by any of his predecessors. He had to reward the deserving, encourage the desponding, temper the zeal of the too confident, replenish and protect the

treasury, claim the services and the blood of new
levies, and carry on, often upon his own responsibility, a war the most gigantic in the history of the
world. Who could wonder that he made occasional
errors, or that the people sometimes complained of
his policy?

But when his course was passed upon by the
people, his re-election proved to the North that his
general policy was sanctioned, and that they were
ready to carry on the war if it lasted four years
longer, aye, or forty years longer—until the great
result was gained.

It proved to the South that there was no escape
for them in empty truce or hollow compromise, that
Lincoln had promised that he would repossess our
forts, and public places, and restore every star to
our flag, and that promise was about to be fulfilled.
Lincoln was re-elected! Sherman was advancing,
Grant stood firm before Richmond, after refusing
to recognise defeat, and the Anaconda was winding itself slowly around the body of the Beast.

At length came the crowning success, Richmond
had fallen! and Lincoln was in person in the rebel
capital, intent, with the generous impulse of a noble
heart, to check the carnage and protect the fallen
foe. Scarcely returned from that mission of mercy,
the felon blow was struck, which calls forth a
Nation's Grief.

Had he fallen by the hand of an unyielding rebel, on his entry into the capital, there would have been some palliation for the act in the voluntary risk he assumed, but to strike him unarmed and unprotected, in the bosom of his family, in a place of amusement, where he had gone as a simple American citizen, unprotected by the guard his rank could have claimed, and the value of his life to the people required, was to take advantage of his confiding nature, and in his act the assassin displayed the utter baseness and depravity of his nature, and the horrible teachings of the fallen cause be sought to sustain by Murder.

It will be said, sir, that his act was not justified by the whole Southern people, and there will doubtless be those there who will denounce it as a crime and despise the assassin, but there will be many to exult in Lincoln's fall, and would be more if he had not lived to inaugurate measures of forgiveness which they will fear his successor may not carry out. The claim of the South to represent the second age of Chivalry has departed. A gentle heart was as necessary to it as gentle blood. Such a heart beat in the bosom of Abraham Lincoln, and it beat long enough after humbling the haughty and setting their bondsmen free, in turn to temper his treatment to the vanquished with mercy and allow his captives to depart in safety, each with the free gift of his charger and his sword. Chivalry had no nobler achievement or more gentle courtesy than this! Contrast with it the Libby Prison and the prison pens of the remote South, where our brother members have participated in Southern hospitality! They were not arranged after the fashion of chivalric receptions of a fallen foe! There was little of chivalry in the massacre at Fort Pillow. We have no record of threats to "cut out the hearts," no minute descriptions of curious knives to "disembowel" an adversary, no shell hidden in coal bunkers, no theory of starving a captured foeman into a noncombatant, in the pages of Froissart or Monstrelet. It is to the savage teaching of Secession and not of Chivalry, that we are indebted, that we have to-day a wide house of mourning in our Land, and a Martyred successor of Washington in our Annals.

On behalf of the Committee, I offer the following resolutions:

Whereas, Providence has permitted in its Wisdom that the President of the United States should fall by an assassin's blow, aimed at the dignity of the Nation : the Athenæum Club, recognizing the loss which they have sustained in common with their fellow-citizens, do

Resolve : That we recognise in the life of our lamented Chief Magistrate, the patient and untiring efforts of a noble, magnanimous and patriotic heart to restore to its integrity a Nation over which it was his fortune to be called to Preside when divided and torn by a rebellion more savage and vindictive than any known in the history of the world, and that in his death we have witnessed a Martyrdom to those efforts which turned against his life the fangs of the serpent which he had torn from the heart of his country.

That, in his efforts to achieve this great work, he has displayed a patriotic perseverance and an ardent desire to restore the Union with as little distress as was practicable, even to those misguided men who, from motives of personal ambition, have striven, with a fiendish malignity, to destroy what their fathers created.

That, at the moment of his death, he had fully accomplished what he had so long struggled for, with varied success, earning a reward only second to that bestowed upon the Father of his Country, and leaving it to his successor to deal with the leaders of this vile conspiracy, and to reorganize and protect their misguided followers under the protection of the old flag.

Resolved ; That in the manner of his death we witness the results of the teachings of secession, and how they have succeeded in " firing the Southern heart," as manifested in the bitter hatred which has been displayed by the rebels in all their acts, and that in the assassination of one so genial, so kindly, and so generous, at the very moment when he was standing between the defeated and prostrate traitors and the indignation of an outraged people, will, when consciousness returns to these misguided men, teach them that they have more to regret in his death than those who have, under the Constitution, recognised his administration and strengthened his hands. As Moses from the top of Pisgah beheld the promised land, he was permitted to view the coming restoration of the Union of the States and the Triumph of the Laws, for which he had patiently labored through four tempestuous years, before his eyes were closed in death.

Resolved ; That we tender the expression of our deep sympathy to the family of the late President and to our fellow-citizens.

Resolved ; That the Club House be draped in Black, and that the members wear the ordinary badge of mourning for thirty days.

Resolved ; That we tender our profound sympathy to the Secretary of State, and to the Assistant Secretary, in the dastardly assault committed upon them, and our contempt for the cowardice manifested in attacking a man while confined to a bed of sickness ; and we trust that Providence will speedily restore them to health and to their Patriotic duties.

Mr. PARKE GODWIN, in seconding the resolutions, said :

Mr. PRESIDENT AND GENTLEMEN:

How grand and how glorious, yet how terrible, the times in which we are permitted to live! How profound and various the emotions that alternately depress and thrill our hearts, like these April skies—now all smiles, and now all tears. Within a week—the Holy Week, as it is called in the Rubrics of our churches—we have had our Triumphal entries, amid the waving of the palms of Peace ; we have had our dread Friday of Crucifixion ; we have had, too, in the recently renewed Patriotism of the Nation, a resurrection of a new and better life! [Sensation.]

It seems but a day or two since we listened to the music of the glad and festive parade ; we saw the Banners of our pride waving with beauty in every air, their Stars bright as the stars of the morning, and their rays of white and red, like the beams of the rainbow, telling that the tempest was past. We pressed hands and hurrahed, and grew almost delirious

with the joy that Peace had come, that Unity was
secured, that Liberty and Justice, like the cheru-
bim of the Ark, would stretch their wings over the
altars of our country, and stand forever as the guar-
dian angels of her sanctity and glory. [Applause.]
But now these exultant strains are changed into
the dull and heavy toll of bells; those flags are
folded and draped in the emblems of Mourning;
and our hearts, giving forth no more the cheering
shouts of Victory, are despondent and full of sadness.

The great Captain of our cause—the Commander-
in-Chief of our armies and navies—the President of
our civic councils—the centre and director of move-
ments—this true son of the People—once the poor
flat-boatman—the village lawyer that was—the raw,
uncouth, yet unsophisticated child of our American
society and institutions, whom that society and those
institutions had lifted out of his low estate to the
foremost dignity of the world—ABRAHAM LINCOLN—
smitten by the basest hand ever upraised against
human innocence, is gone, gone, gone! He who
had borne the heaviest of the brunt, in our four
long years of war, whose pulse beat livelier, whose
eyes danced brighter than any others, when

———— " the storm drew off
In scattered thunders groaning round the hills."

in the supreme hour of his joy and glory was struck
down. That genial, kindly heart has ceased to beat;

that noble brain has oozed from its mysterious beds; that manly form lies still in Death's icy fetters, and all of him that was mortal has sunk "to the portion of weeds and outworn faces." [Sensation.]

Our feelings are now too deep to ask or warrant any attempt at an analysis of the character of the services of the man whose loss we deplore. Standing over his bier, looking down almost into the tomb to which he must shortly be consigned, we are conscious only of our grief. We know that one who was great in himself, as well as by position, has suddenly departed. There is something startling, ghastly, awful in the manner of his going off. But the chief poignancy of our distress is not for greatness fallen, but for the goodness lost. Presidents have died before; during this bloody war we have lost many eminent generals — Lyons, Baker, Kearney, Sedgwick, Mitchell, and others; we have lost lately our finest scholar, publicist, orator,

> —— "that when he spoke,
> The air, a chartered libertine, was still,
> 'To steal his sweet and honeyed sentences.'"

Our hearts still bleed for the companions, friends, brothers that sleep the sleep "that knows no waking," but no loss has been comparable to his, who was our supremest Leader—our safest Counsellor—our wisest Friend—our dear Father. Would you know what LINCOLN was, look at this vast metropolis, covered with the habiliments of woe! Never in human history has there been so universal, so spontaneous, so profound an expression of a Nation's bereavement. In all our churches, without distinction of sect; in all our journals, without distinction of party; in all our workshops, in all our counting houses—from the stateliest mansion to the lowliest hovel—you hear but the one utterance, you see but the one emblem of sorrow. Why has the death of Abraham Lincoln taken such deep hold of every class? Partly, no doubt, because of the awful and atrocious method of his death; partly because he was our Chief Magistrate; but, mainly, I think, because through all his public functions there shone the fact that he was a wise and good man; a kindly, honest, noble man; a man in whom the people recognised their own better qualities; whom they, whatever their political convictions, trusted; whom they respected; whom they loved; a man as pure of heart, as patriotic of impulse, as patient, gentle, sweet and lovely of nature, as ever history lifted out of the sphere of the domestic affections to enshrine forever in the affections of the world. [Loud and continuous applause.]

Yet, we sorrow not as those who are without hope. Our Chief has gone, but our cause remains; dearer to our hearts, because he is now become its martyr; consecrated by his sacrifice; more widely accepted by all parties; and fragrant and lovely forevermore in the memories of all the good and the great of all lands, and for all time. The rebellion, which began in the blackest treachery, to be ended in the foulest assassination; for, as Shakespeare says,

" Treason and murder ever kept together.
As two yoke-devils sworn to either's purpose."

this rebellion, accursed in its motive, which was to rivet the shackles of slavery on a whole race for all the future; accursed in its means, which have been "red ruin and the breaking up of laws," the overthrow of the mildest and blessedest of governments, and the profuse shedding of brother's blood by brother's hands; accursed in its accompaniments of violence, cruelty, and barbarism, is now doubly accursed in its final act of cold-blooded murder. [Applause.]

Cold-blooded! but impotent, and defeated in its own purposes. The frenzied hand which slew the head of the government, in the mad hope of paralyzing its functions, only drew the hearts of the people together more closely to strengthen and sustain its power. All the North once more, without party or division, clenches hands around the common altar; all the North swears a more earnest fidelity to freedom; all the North again presents its breasts, as the living shield and bulwark of the nation's unity and life. Oh! foolish and wicked dream. Oh! insanity of fanaticism, Oh! blindness of black hate—to think that this majestic temple of human liberty, with its clustered columns of free and prosperous states, and whose base is as broad as the continent—could be shaken to pieces by striking off the ornaments of its capital! No! this Nation lives, not in one man nor in a hundred men, however eminent, however able, however endeared to us; but in the affections, the virtues, the energies, and the will of the whole American people. It has perpetual succession, not like a Dynasty in the line of its rulers, but in the line of its masses. They are always alive; they are always present to empower its acts and to impart an unceasing vitality to its institutions. No maniac's blade, no traitor's bullet shall ever penetrate that heart, for it is immortal, like the substance of Milton's angels, and can only "by annihilating die." [Applause.]

These sudden visitations of Providence; these mysterious and fearful vicissitudes in the destinies of nations and individuals, always seem to our shortsighted human wisdom as inscrutable. Nor would it be less than presumption in any one to attempt to interpret the meaning of the Divine Mind in this late and most appalling affliction. God, as he passes, the Scriptures tell us, can only be seen from behind, can only be seen when events have gone by. Until then we grope in the darkness, we guess at best but dimly, we more often muse in mere mute wonder and awe. Yet it is always permitted us to extract such good as we may from his seeming frowns and judgments. Thus I discern, in the removal of Mr. Lincoln—lamentable and horrible as it was in its circumstances—some reasons for a calm and hopeful submission to the Divine Will. I can see how our nation is cemented by its tears into a more universal and affectionate brotherhood; I can see how the Proclamation of Freedom must become the eternal law of our hearts, if not of the land, through the martyrdom and canonization of its author; I can see how the atrocious crime of assassination must tear away from the rebellion every friend that it had left in the civilized world abroad; and I can see how the succession of Mr. Johnson—a Southern man, known to the Southern people by the fact of his origin and principles, not amenable to the prejudices knotted and gnarled about Mr. Lincoln—shall undermine the supremacy of the Southern leaders and reconcile the deluded masses more rapidly than any acts of amnesty or promises of forgiveness. [Cheers.]

But what impresses me most forcibly in all this business is, the new demonstration that it has given of the inherent strength and elasticity of democratic government. We have conducted the most stupendous war ever undertaken—a war that involved the blockade of six thousand miles of seacoast—the defence of two thousand miles of frontier—the clearing and holding of the second largest river of the globe, and the occupation of a territory greater than all Europe (with-

out Russia) not only energetically, but successfully
We have done it without abandoning, or vitiating, or
dislocating any of our fundamental institutions. For
in the midst of this gigantic convulsion, we carried on
a political canvass and a Presidential election as qui-
etly as they choose a beadle or a churchwarden else-
where; and now we have our principal men of office
killed or disabled, and the government goes on without a jar, and society moves in its appointed way
without a ripple of outbreak or disorder. Oh! yes,
Americans, our good ship of State, which the tempests
assail with their wild fury, which the angry surges
lift in their arms, that they may drop her into the
yawning gulf, which the treacherous hidden rocks
below grind and torture, yet sails on securely to her
destined port; and when the very Prince of the Power
of the Air smites her Captain at the helm, and the
first mate in his berth, she still sails on securely to her
destined port: for her crew is still there: they know
her bearings and will steer right on by the compass
of Eternal justice, and under the celestial light of
Liberty.

Mr. GEORGE P. PUTNAM sustained the resolutions,
as follows:

Mr. PRESIDENT: It may be presumptuous, especially
for one who has no power as a speaker, to add any-

thing to the eloquent and forcible remarks of the gentlemen who have already spoken. I would with deference merely refer to one or two thoughts which have been already expressed.

Mr. Godwin has well said, that even in this overwhelming calamity and amidst this deeply affecting spectacle of a great nation in tears, for the loss of its loved and honored chief, we do not sorrow as those who have no hope. May it not be, sir, that the beneficent Ruler of the Universe has permitted this heavy blow to be struck for His own wise and merciful purposes of permanent good to this nation; that this crowning bereavement, like many lesser disasters throughout the great struggle of these troublous and fruitful years, may prove to have been needful for our national salvation and national purification? May it not prove that there was danger of too much leniency and forbearance to traitors, and that God would teach us that Justice must not be wholly superseded even by benignant Mercy? Is not our new President right, in saying that in the present position of this nation, indulgence to leading traitors may be cruelty to the State?

For one, sir, I must confess a mortal repugnance to bloody revenge, and I believe the worst use you can make of a man is to hang him. I would give full force to all those considerations, which are rightly urged against vindictive retaliation even for

the crimes of the authors and leaders of this foul
rebellion. The spirit of our Saviour's teachings
should govern this people as well as the law from
Mount Sinai. But, sir, what can any one of us ask
or expect of our government in disposing of the
responsible leaders of the late audacious and wicked
conspiracy against the life of a nation—the tortur-
ers and butchers of our prisoners, and the authors,
at least of the *teachings* which have prompted the
attempt at midnight murder of thousands of peace-
able women and children in our cities, and now the
dastardly assassination of the great and good Chief
of the nation? Can we expect that these criminals
(wherever the difficult line may be drawn) shall
suffer less than permanent expatriation from the
land they have steeped in blood and covered with
the graves of tens of thousands of martyrs to their
unholy, selfish, reckless ambition?

If we say nothing of the shining marks—the
nobler victims of the war itself—the Ellsworths, the
Lowells, the Sedgwicks, the Winthrops, the Wads-
worths, who have fallen in the field—can we again
welcome to honorable citizenship, the men who either
directed or countenanced the doings at Fort Pillow,
at Lawrence, at Salisbury, and Andersonville?

Sir, we are glad to believe, whatever may have
been previous impressions, that in our new President we have a man of nerve, of integrity, and

of ability, who will not shrink from the duties devolving upon him,. but will administer justice in no spirit of mean revenge, but as the executive agent of a great people who have earned by their best blood, the right, under God's blessing, of future security and permanent peace.

We are willing to believe that he, too, as well as his martyred predecessor, has been fitted by the Almighty—over and above all defects of education or the personal associations of a slave-state — for the momentous duties of the hour upon which depends the future of this continent.

Glance back a few years—nay a few months. The suggestions of experience, the wonderful teachings of Providence, which crowd upon us as we look at past events, would fill volumes. I do not presume to detain you. But just think of ABRAHAM LINCOLN, legally, rightfully chosen though he was, for his high office—yet obliged to reach the Capital almost as a fugitive in disguise. Think of the then current jeers about " Old Abe the rail-splitter"—" the buffoon"—" the ape," not so-called only by Southern rebels, but openly in the streets of New York—think of the amazing task which lay before this untried lawyer of a Western village—think of his difficulties and discouragements—not from open foes alone, but from professed friends—his own party supporters almost deserting

4

him as unequal to the crisis, and calling for "a Dictator." Think of the fact that his wisdom and ability were thus doubted, not merely in the first year of repulses and disasters, but that even within the last eight months, some of the most active republicans were busily planning to supersede him as the "weakest candidate" for the succession; consider the harassing pressure upon him by visionary or selfish friends, for widely opposite and variously doubtful schemes of public policy—consider his calm patience, his quiet energy—his modest and kindly bearing to all—his sublime and enduring faith in the God of justice and of mercy! And now that his bodily presence with us has ceased forever, look around and see this great city—nay, almost every habitation in the land, literally draped in mourning—not dictated by Imperial edict, but the spontaneous symbol of a deep and earnest sorrow — shared, let us believe, sincerely, by thousands who had hitherto reviled while they secretly must have respected and admired this true "man of the people." Observe men of all shades of opinion and faith lauding his virtues, doing homage to his noble patriotism, his immortal services to the people he loved so well!

Has any one of us walked our streets since Saturday, without having the tears rise unbidden at these spontaneous tokens of heartfelt affection and respect

for our late President ? Has the world ever seen a
spectacle more touching, more worthy of a free
people ? Suppose he had lived a few weeks longer
to see the full consummation of that glad time,
when the old flag waving in every city and village
over the broad land, is again acknowledged and
respected and loved as the symbol of a great Na-
tionality, governed by the eternal principles of justice, and enjoying the blessings of freedom, in peace
and prosperity. Suppose this new era had fully
dawned, and Abraham Lincoln, the rail-splitter, had
again visited our great cities, what would have
been his reception ? But he was permitted to reach
only the near view of this glorious result of all
his patient toil and quiet faith, now so well assured.

It has been well said, also, by Mr. Godwin, that
this event leaves a great lesson, and a cause for
national gratitude amidst our grief, in the proof it
has given the world of the stability of our institutions. Shrewd and judicious, though, perhaps, over-
timid men feared at first, that a blow so startling
must be followed by distrust, confusion, anarchy.
But the wheels of government have moved steadily
and serenely on ; the " gold " thermometer of Wall
street was scarcely disturbed by a fraction, and on
the Saturday which proclaimed the national calamity, and while the nation was almost paralyzed
with horror at the parricide, the nation's popular

loan received larger subscriptions than ever before!
The confidence of the people was firm and unshaken.
Well may we look at the bow of promise, even
now visible over the heavy cloud of affliction! Well
may we believe that the tears now mingled over
the bier of the last great victim of the expiring
monsters, Slavery and Treason, with the blood of
the noble army of martyrs who have gone before,
will together unite the hearts of this great people,
purified and renovated, and rising, as in the resurrection morning, to a future life of happiness and
peace. For well is it already written of Abraham
Lincoln—

> —— " His patient toil
> Has robed our cause in Victory's light :
> Our country stood redeemed and bright,
> With not a slave upon her soil.
>
> " A Martyr to the cause of man,
> His blood is Freedom's Eucharist,
> And in the world's great hero-list
> His name shall lead the van."

Mr. W. CARY SMITH followed with these remarks :

Mr. PRESIDENT : I have a natural hesitancy in rising to speak at such a time, while your minds are
still under the spell of the eloquent words to which
you have just listened. But as it has been thought
well that there should be some expression on the
part of the younger members of the Club, I beg
your indulgence for a moment.

Sir, the President of the United States has fallen by the hand of an assassin. Such an announcement needs no remarks. For a period of two hundred and twenty-five years no such event has occurred. For the first time in all the many vehement and heated struggles of our national history, political animosity and partisan hate, defeated at the ballot-box and in the field, has vented its baffled rage in the perpetration of a crime, at which the Civilization of the age stands appalled, a crime against humanity and Christianity, against man and against God.

This is no natural out-growth of our American institutions. But it becomes us as citizens of a common country to consider well, whether there be anything in the social organization of any portion of it, favorable to the engendering of such a moral monster as the doer of this deed, any habits of thought, of action, any tone of feeling pervading a community of which this crowning iniquity is a legitimate expression. I desire to avoid offence, but, sir, as a Southerner by birth, I maintain, and it cannot be denied, that there is a portion of this land, whose leaders, grown rich on the unrequited toil of bondsmen, yet claiming to be a chivalric nation of gentlemen, have openly advocated this deed, the very shadow of whose monstrous iniquity darkens the heavens.

It cannot be denied that this assassin can look for approval, for aid, for protection, in no part of Christendom, save in the limits of that section of the Union so recently in rebellion against the government.

The responsibility of this crime is justly chargable upon the South. Their so-called domestic institutions and their leaders, stand to-day arraigned at the bar of the civilized world as criminal against the rights of mankind.

It is our duty to see to it that the last vestige of this barbarism be eradicated. We owe it to ourselves, to posterity, to liberty, never to pause, to rest, nor to falter, till the land be purged.

In view of the humble origin of the late President, of his upright character, his inestimable services, let no man despair of the safety of this Republic. The unbroken civil order maintained during the shock which followed his untimely death, fully vindicates the majesty of Popular government.

The blow which reft his life, dissipated in an instant the vapors of prejudice and partisan misrepresentations which endeavored to impede his progress. His place in history is henceforth secure, the memory of his just deeds immortal.

His body mingles with the sacred ashes of those over whom a nation watches with jealous, loving care. His spirit has gone to lead the van of that

long triumphant procession of heroes and martyrs
of liberty, who, in all the pomp and circumstance of
a militant faith, have passed through the portals of
time into the light of perfect day.

Mr. FRANCIS A. STOUT made the following remarks in regard to a significant fact connected
with the last hours of Mr. LINCOLN. Mr. STOUT
said :

An incident has come to my knowledge which,
at this sad time, is of unusual interest.

About ten days since, one of our members, General VAN ALEN, became, even more than ever,
profoundly impressed with the inestimable value
to the country, at this peculiar juncture of public
affairs, of the life of ABRAHAM LINCOLN, the wisest
and best of contemporary Americans.

Under the impulse of an uncontrollable and
almost prophetic anxiety, he then wrote to the
President, urging him to guard his life with greater
care, that his personal security might suffer no
detriment from rebel knife or bullet, and that the
nation might be assured of its own safety by
contemplating his.

On Friday last, the day when he was to be
added to the noble army of martyrs who have
died for freedom and for man, the President dis·

patched to General VAN ALEN a letter of considerable length, in which, after touching upon topics of public and private concern, he stated his intention to use, hereafter, "due precautionary measures." Mr. President, I can make no comment.

The resolutions were then unanimously adopted.

Mr. JOHN II. WHITE then arose and said, that while the proceedings of the evening would be noted upon the records of the Club, he deemed it eminently fit and proper that the outside world should know the horror and detestation with which the members of the Club looked upon the fiendish crime which had filled the land with mourning. The assassination of the President of the United States, and the attempted assassination of the Secretary of State, in its heinousness and enormity had no historic precedent or parallel. It stands solitary and alone; language being inadequate to give it a fitting and proper name; and it can only be accounted for as an emanation from, and the legitimate fruit of SLAVERY, SECESSION, TREASON, and the FIEND INCARNATE. He did not intend to take up the time of the Club by further remarks, but he hoped the mover of the resolutions, which had been adopted with such unanimity, would furnish copies of the same, to be published with the other proceedings of the Club.

After the adoption of the resolution the meeting adjourned.

GEORGE V. N. BALDWIN,

Secretary.

ODE.

Written by Mr. HENRY T TUCKERMAN, of the Committee on Resolutions, for the funeral obsequies, April 25, 1865

I.

Shroud the Banner! rear the Cross!
Consecrate a Nation's loss;
Gaze on that majestic sleep,
Stand beside the bier to weep;
Lay the gentle son of toil
Proudly in his native soil;
Crowned with honor, to his rest
Bear the Prophet of the West!

II.

How cold the brow that yet doth wear
The impress of a Nation's care;
How still the heart whose every beat
Glowed with compassion's sacred heat;
Rigid the lips whose patient smile
Duty's stern task would oft beguile;
Blood-quenched the pensive eye's soft light,
Nerveless the hand so loath to smite,
So meek in rule, it leads, though dead,
The People as in life it led.

III.

O! let his wise and guileless sway
Win every recreant to-day,
And sorrow's vast and holy wave
Blend all our hearts around his grave!
Let the faithful bondsmen's tears,
Let the traitor's craven fears,
And the people's grief and pride
Plead against the parricide!
Let us throng to pledge and pray
O'er the patriot-martyr's clay;
Then with solemn faith in Right,
That made him victor in the fight,
Cling to the path he fearless trod
Still radiant with the smile of God.

IV.

Shroud the Banner! rear the Cross!
Consecrate a Nation's loss!
Gaze on that majestic sleep,
Stand beside the bier to weep;
Lay the gentle son of toil
Proudly in his native soil;
Crowned with honor, to his rest
Bear the Prophet of the West!

IN the funeral obsequies on the 25th of April, the Athenæum Club participated, bearing an appropriate banner, the members wearing distinctive badges of mourning, and headed by their Vice-President, Mr. HENRY E. PIERREPONT, the President, Mr. WILLIAM T. BLODGETT, being then absent, as Chairman of the Citizens' Committee.